P9-CQE-791

WHO iNViTED YOU?

by CANDACE FLEMING pictures by GEORGE BOOTH

AN ANNE SCHWARTZ BOOK
Atheneum Books for Young Readers

New York London Toronto Sydney Singapore

To Anne Schwartz, for never being afraid to let the gators loose
—C. F.

For Sarah, my gator daughter
—G. B.

Atheneum Books for Young Readers
An imprint of Simon & Schuster Children's Publishing Division
1230 Avenue of the Americas
New York, New York 10020

Text copyright © 2001 by Candace Fleming
Illustrations copyright © 2001 by George Booth

Book design by Ann Bobco
The text of this book is set in Garamond Berthold Medium.
The illustrations are rendered in ink and watercolor.

Printed in Hong Kong

10 9 8 7 6 5 4 3 2 1

Library of Congress Cataloging-in-Publication Data

Fleming, Candace.
Who invited you? / by Candace Fleming ; illustrated by George Booth. — 1st ed.
p. cm.
Summary: A rhyming counting tale in which Possum, Skunk, Frog, and other animals join a procession
through the swamp, one with a potentially dangerous conclusion.
ISBN 0-689-83153-6
[1. Animals Fiction. 2. Swamps Fiction. 3. Counting. 4. Stories in rhyme.] I. Booth, George, 1926- ill. II. Title.
PZ8.3.F63775Cr 2001
[E]—dc21
99-27028

I was a-polin' through the swamp,

only one,

only me,

when I came to the place filled with moss-covered trees.

Possum was there . . .

a-swingin',

a-swayin',

a-dangly-wangly-playin'.

"Whoo-eee!" whooped he.

"I'm a-comin' along!"

And he dropped from the tree,

 right on top of me.

"Hey!" I hollered. "Who invited you?"

"If you got room for one," said Possum,

"you got room for two."

So we became two,

a-feelin' just fine,

when I poled past a snarl of ferns, shrubs, and vines.

Skunk was there . . .

a-sprayin',

a-sprinklin',

a-wavey-tavey-tinklin'.

"Pinch your noses," warned he.

"I'm a-comin' along."

And he sprang from the shore,

right on top of me.

"Scat!" cried Possum.

"No critters ride but me!"

"If you got room for two," said Skunk,

"you got room for three."

So we became three,

a right cozy fit,

when I poled through the shade where the lilies grow thick.

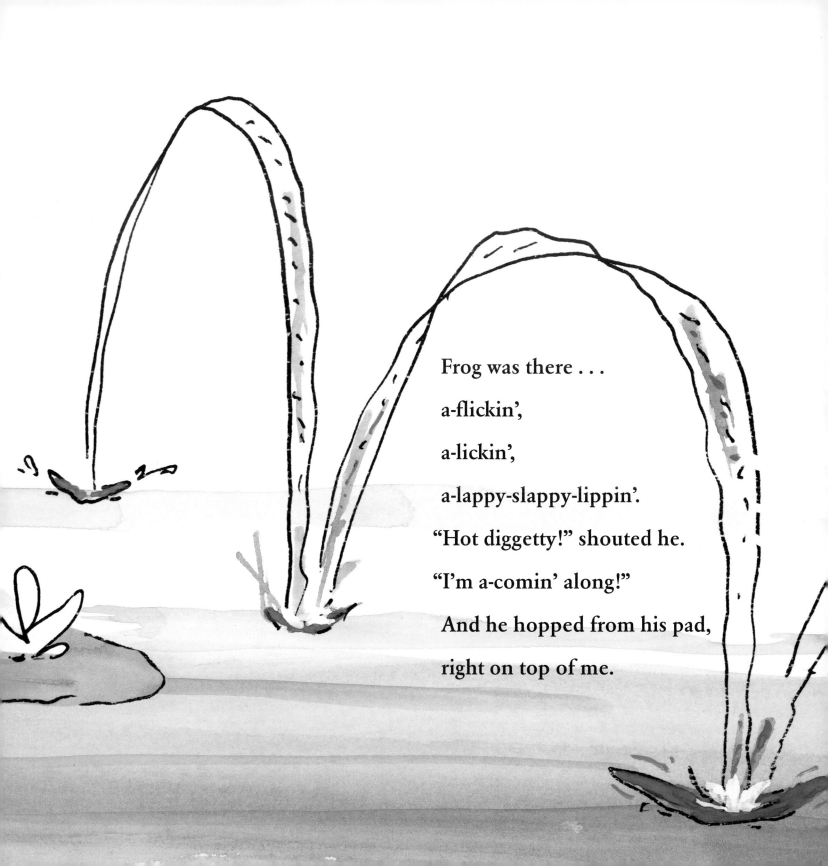

Frog was there . . .

a-flickin',

a-lickin',

a-lappy-slappy-lippin'.

"Hot diggetty!" shouted he.

"I'm a-comin' along!"

And he hopped from his pad,

right on top of me.

"Be gone!" sniffed Skunk.

"We don't want no more!"

"If you got room for three," said Frog,

"you got room for four."

So we became four,

a little bit snug,

when I poled between bushes where blueberries hung.

Muskrat was there . . .

a-pickin',

a-stoppin',

a-sticky-picky-poppin'.

"Me! Me!" squealed he.

"I'm a-comin' along!"

And he scrambled from the bushes,

right on top of me.

"Get out!" croaked Frog.

"Land's sakes alive!"

"If you got room for four," said Muskrat,

"you got room for five."

So we became five,
a-startin' to squeeze,
when I poled through a mess
of marsh grass and weeds.

Heron was there . . .

a-flappin',

a-floppin',

a-hippy-happy-hoppin'.

"O-ho," hooted she.

"I'm a-comin' along."

And she swooped from the grass,

right on top of me.

"Stay off!" screeched Muskrat.

"We can't ride like this!"

"If you got room for five," said Heron,

"you got room for six."

So we became six,
mighty packed in,
when I poled round the hole where the big catfish swim.

Coon was there . . .

a-splishin',

a-splashin',

a-fishy-wishy-catchin'.

"Scoot over," snarled he.

"I'm a-comin' along."

And he waddled from the water,

right on top of me.

"Fly away!" piped Heron.

"Or we'll knock you clean to heaven!"

"If you got room for six," said Coon,

"you got room for seven."

So we became seven,

crowded in close,

when I poled down the channel

where the water oaks grow.

Beaver was there . . .

a-sawin',

a-clawin',

a-nibbly-nabbly-gnawin'.

"Wait for me!" howled he.

"I'm a-comin' along."

And he paddled from his dam,

right on top of me.

"Beat it!" called Coon.

"You're a-makin' a mistake."

"If you got room for seven," said Beaver,

"you got room for eight."

So we became eight,

hardly able to breathe,

when I poled past a mudbank beyond those tall trees.

Otter was there . . .

a-floppin',

a-flippin',

a-sloppy-ploppy-slippin'.

"Tee hee!" giggled he.

"I'm a-comin' along."

And he whooshed down the bank,

right on top of me.

"Scram!" screamed Beaver.

"You ain't welcome at this time."

"If you got room for eight," said Otter,

"you got room for nine."

Now we are nine,

not an inch more of space,

as we enter the waters of cold, dark Swamp Lake.

Gator is here . . .

a-smilin',

a-slinkin',

a-blinky-blanky-winkin'.

"Mmmm! Mmmm!" drawls he.

"I'm a-comin' along."

And he crawls from the water, right on top of me.

"Out!" scolds Possum. "This really will not do!"

"Ten's too many," we all cry.

"There ain't no room for you!"

"That's all right," Gator grins,

" 'cause I have room for . . .

Now I'm only one,

a-feelin' just fine . . .

. . . and I pole

only ME

through the bright swamp sunshine.